Animal Groups

by Kristen Kunkel

HOUGHTON MIFFLIN HARCOURT

brown animals

big animals

Animals are living things.
We can sort animals into groups.
One way to group them is by how they look.

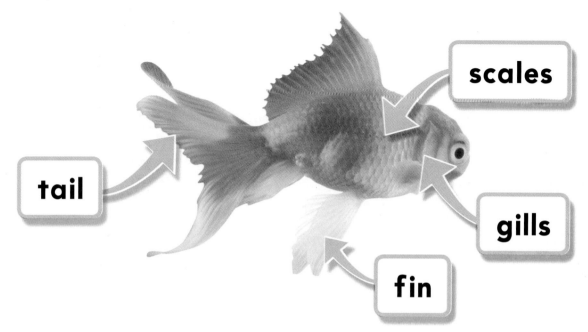

scales

tail

gills

fin

Scientists sort animals by body parts.
Fish are a group of animals.
Fish have gills to breathe water.

feathers

beak

wing

Birds are a group of animals.
Birds have feathers.
They have a beak and wings.

live young

fur

Mammals are a group of animals.
Mammals have fur or hair.
Most mammals have live young.

scales

Reptiles are a group of animals. Reptiles have dry skin that is covered with scales.

lives in water

gills

young frog

lives on land

has lungs

adult frog

Amphibians are a group of animals.
Many amphibians have smooth, wet skin.
Their body parts change as they grow.

Sort Animals

Draw ten different animals. Then sort the animals into the groups you learned about in this book. Make labels for each of the groups. Then pair up with a partner to compare and then combine your animals and groups.

Identify Body Parts

Draw a picture of your favorite animal. Then label at least five of the animal's body parts. Finally, write the following sentence frame, filling in the blanks with the name of your animal and the appropriate animal group from the book.

A(n) _____ is a(n) _____.

Vocabulary

amphibians	lungs
feathers	mammals
fur	reptiles
gills	scales
living things	